Big Bill's Beltie Bairns

Written by Jayne Baldwin

Illustrated by Shalla Gray

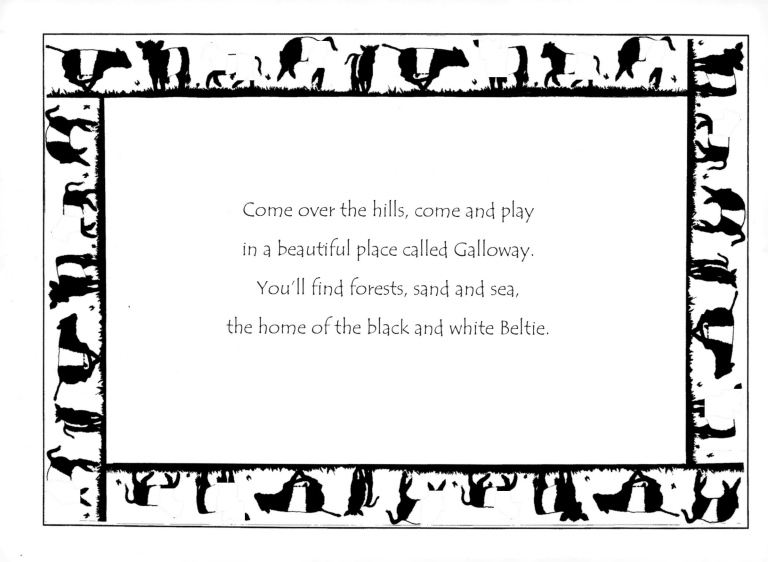

Come over the hills, come and play

in a beautiful place called Galloway.

You'll find forests, sand and sea,

the home of the black and white Beltie.

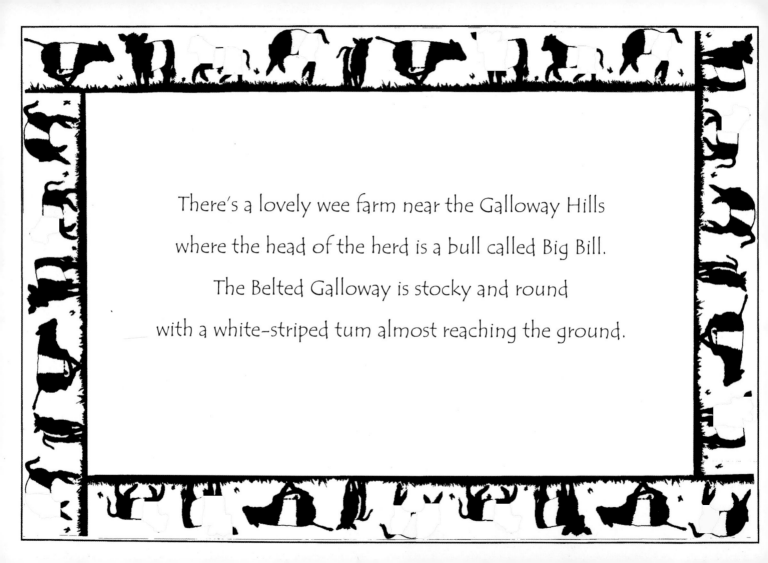

There's a lovely wee farm near the Galloway Hills

where the head of the herd is a bull called Big Bill.

The Belted Galloway is stocky and round

with a white-striped tum almost reaching the ground.

One Winter night Bertie and Buntie were born

at Benyellary Farm in a wild snow storm.

They snuggled up warm with their mum in the barn,

outside the wind whirled, but inside all was calm.

But now Winter has gone, and the Spring has arrived,

their mum says its time they should all go outside.

It's a bright Spring day and the Sun's in the sky,

it's a beautiful blue, fluffy clouds floating by.

Mum says they're ready to go join the herd,

Bertie and Buntie are baffled, they think they've misheard.

"There are more Belties than us?" Bertie's very surprised,

Buntie wonders where they found lots of places to hide.

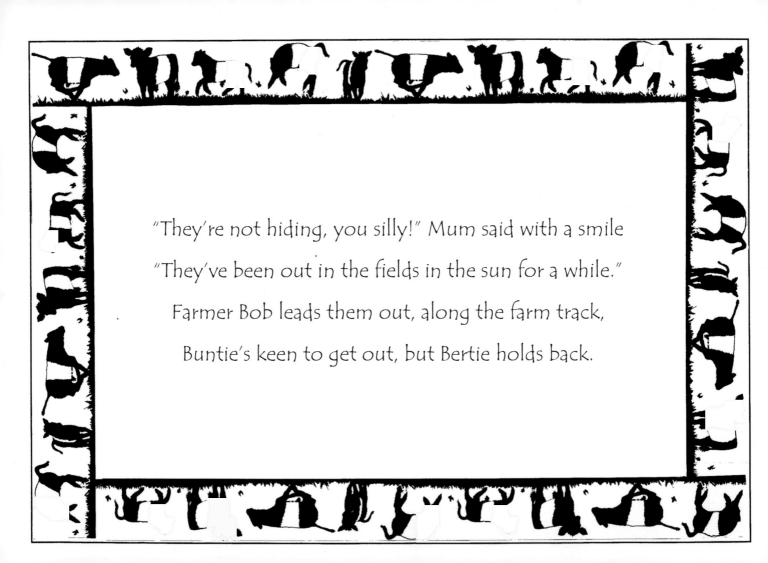

"They're not hiding, you silly!" Mum said with a smile

"They've been out in the fields in the sun for a while."

Farmer Bob leads them out, along the farm track,

Buntie's keen to get out, but Bertie holds back.

He's seen a blue monster with huge, scary jaws,

lots of big shiny eyes and terrifying claws!

"It won't hurt you Bertie," his mum softly says,

"It's used by the farmer to carry the hay."

Then it's off to the meadow where the grass is so green,

but then Buntie stops suddenly; what's that she's seen?

There's a calf just like her, but instead of being black

it's red up at its head and red right at the back.

There's still a big white stripe around the other's tum

but Bertie spots something; there's another one!

This one has no stripe at all; it's white from head to tail.

Perhaps she's ill, not very well, she's looking very pale.

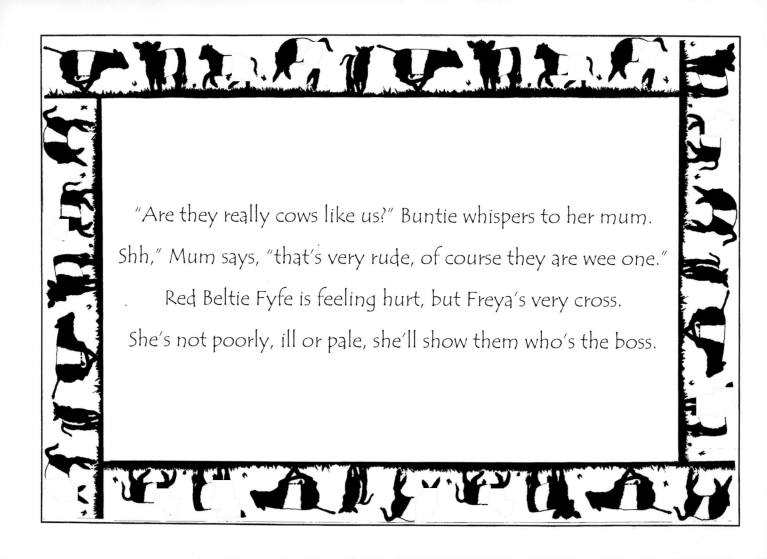

"Are they really cows like us?" Buntie whispers to her mum.

Shh," Mum says, "that's very rude, of course they are wee one."

Red Beltie Fyfe is feeling hurt, but Freya's very cross.

She's not poorly, ill or pale, she'll show them who's the boss.

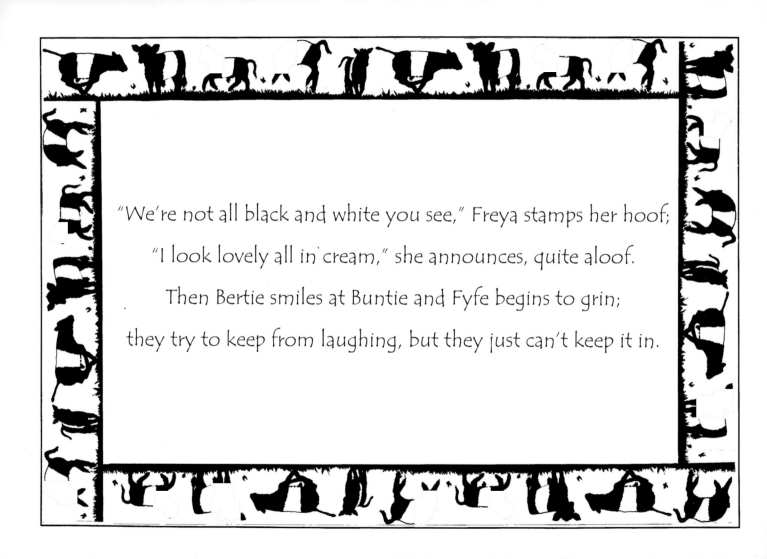

"We're not all black and white you see," Freya stamps her hoof;

"I look lovely all in cream," she announces, quite aloof.

Then Bertie smiles at Buntie and Fyfe begins to grin;

they try to keep from laughing, but they just can't keep it in.

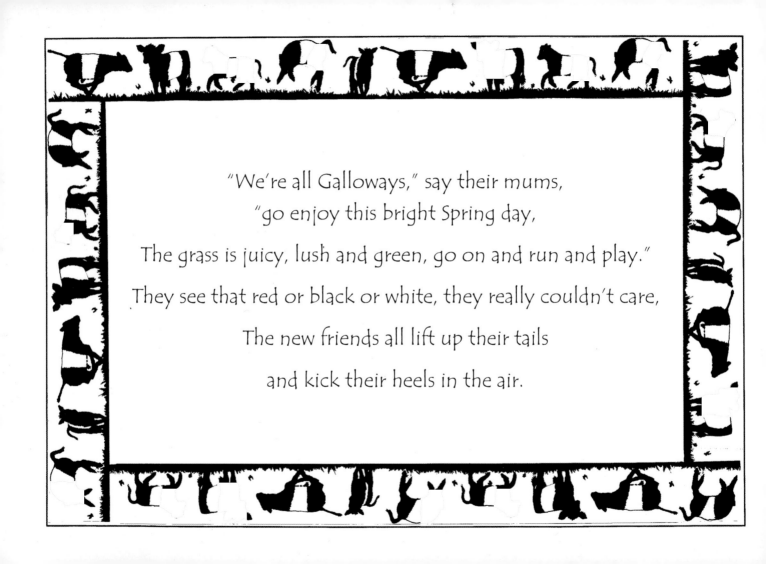

"We're all Galloways," say their mums,
"go enjoy this bright Spring day,

The grass is juicy, lush and green, go on and run and play."

They see that red or black or white, they really couldn't care,

The new friends all lift up their tails

and kick their heels in the air.

Linnet

CAN YOU SPOT THESE ANIMALS AND PLANTS IN THE STORY? Why not go back and spot the snail, the butterfly, the bird and the flower on every page. See if you can keep an eye on Big Bill too!

Song Thrush

Peacock Butterfly

Snail!

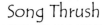
Wild Strawberry

Starling

Small Tortoiseshell

Red Admiral

Pied Wagtail

More Titles From Curly Tale Books:

The Galloway Chilli
Written & Illustrated by Shalla Gray

CURLY TALE BOOKS

Come & visit us in our children's bookshop in Wigtown, Scotland's National Booktown.

maxwell's mega mission
Jayne Baldwin

Big Bill the Beltie Bull
Written & Illustrated by Shalla Gray

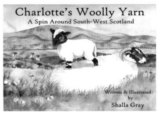

Charlotte's Woolly Yarn
A Spin Around South-West Scotland
Written & Illustrated by Shalla Gray

Sammy the Rainbow Snail
alan grant shalla gray

Big Bill and the Larking Lambs
Written by Jayne Baldwin
Illustrated by Shalla Gray

The Quite Big Rock
Written by Alan Grant
Illustrated by Shalla Gray

Curlytale Books

www.curlytalebooks.co.uk

WORDSEARCH

BIG BILL'S BELTIE BAIRNS

FIND THESE WORDS:

FLOWER	HEN	TRACTOR
CAT	COW	BULL
DOG	BARN	FARM

T	B	W	G	H	F
R	B	U	H	E	L
A	D	L	L	N	O
C	O	W	B	L	W
T	G	C	A	T	E
O	F	A	R	M	R
R	H	T	N	E	B

ISBN: 978-0957-640221
Published by Curly Tale Books Ltd
34 Main Street
Kirkcowan
DG8 0HG
www.curlytalebooks.co.uk
Written by Jayne Baldwin
Illustrated by Shalla Gray

Printed by J&B Print,
32A Albert Street,
Newton Stewart, DG8 6EJ